nickelodeon™ **TEAM UMIZOOMI**™

S0-BXV-789

MIGHTY ADVENTURES

Illustrated by Jason Fruchter

A GOLDEN BOOK • NEW YORK

ISBN: 978-0-307-93085-9
randomhouse.com/kids
Printed in the United States of America
10 9 8 7 6 5 4

Hi, I'm Milli!

That's my brother, Geo, and our best robot friend, Bot!

We're Team Umizoomi!
And we've got Mighty Math Powers!

We're looking at pictures of our friend UmiCar.
Connect the dots to see UmiCar!

UmiCar takes us wherever we want to go.

We love UmiCar!

Oh, no! It's the Umi Alarm! UmiCar is in trouble!
He's stuck far away on Iceberg Bay!

He needs our help! UmiFriend, will you help us save UmiCar?

Team Umizoomi, it's time for action!

To get to Iceberg Bay, we first have to go to the train station and take a train through the mountains. Can you find the station? Color it orange.

The train is missing its engine! We can make
an engine with shapes from my ShapeBelt!
Which shapes can we use?

Now we need to complete the train. Will you connect the dots to make the back of the train?

Super Shapes! UmiFriend, we made a super train!

All aboard the Umi Train!

Oh, no! There's a problem up ahead!
A piece of the train track is missing.

Here are some extra train tracks. We need the longest
curved piece. Which one is it?

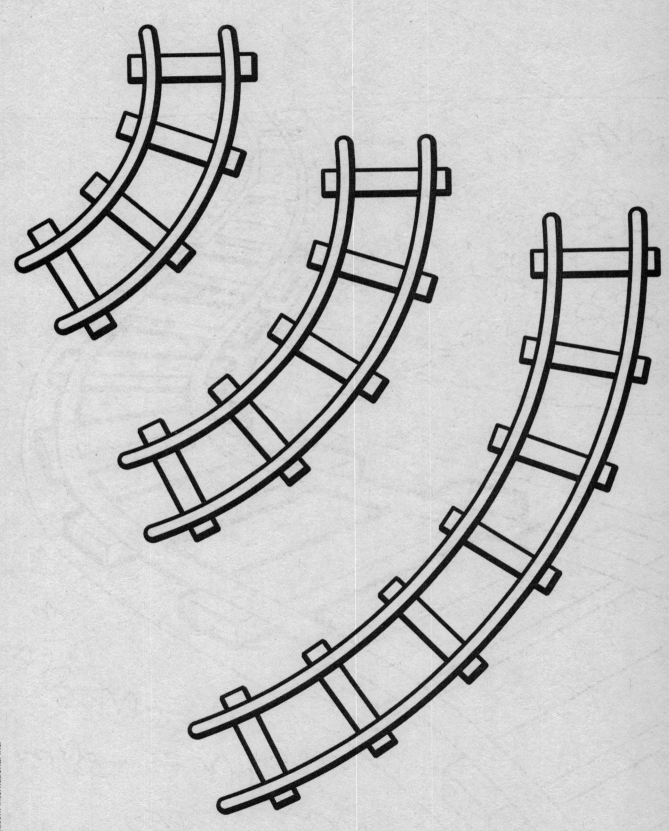

Umirrific! You found it! Now we can go to the mountains.

My Belly, Belly, Bellyscreen says that UmiCar's iceberg is melting! We've got to hurry!

We need a dogsled to take us over the mountain.
Let's use shapes from my ShapeBelt! Can you help find
the shapes that will make the sled?

Let's turn it into a super dogsled! *Super Shapes!*
Great job, UmiFriend!

We say a special word to make Doggie run.
Use this code to find out what it is.

| ❄ = H | 🦴 = M | ⌐ = S | 🐺 = U |

Doggie is hungry. His dog treat has a number on it.
Which treat has the number 1 on it?

Uh-oh! Doggie is slowing down. Can you find the bone with the highest number? The higher the number on the bone, the more energy he will have!

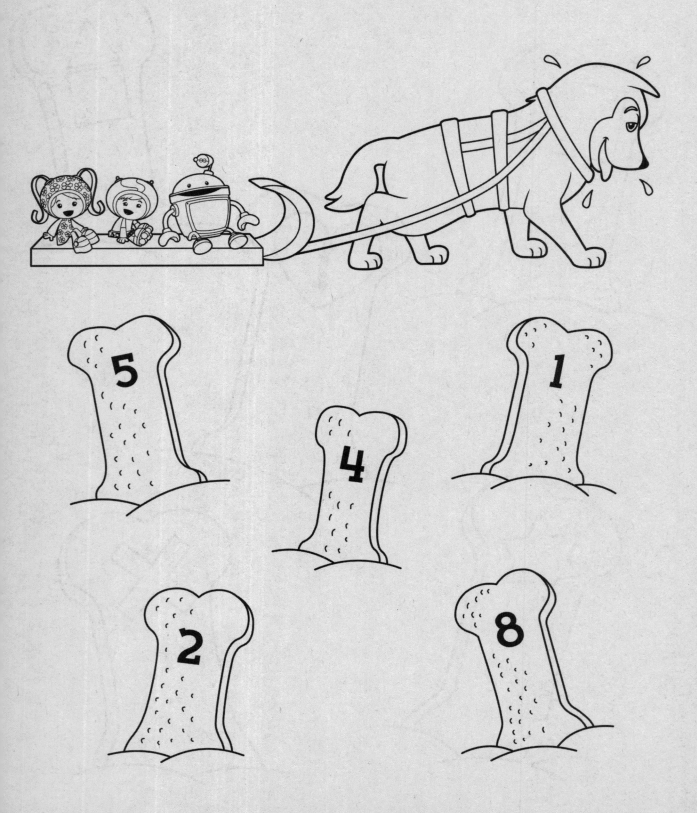

Now we need to take a speedboat to Iceberg Bay.
To make the speedboat, we need a triangle and
a trapezoid. Can you find them?

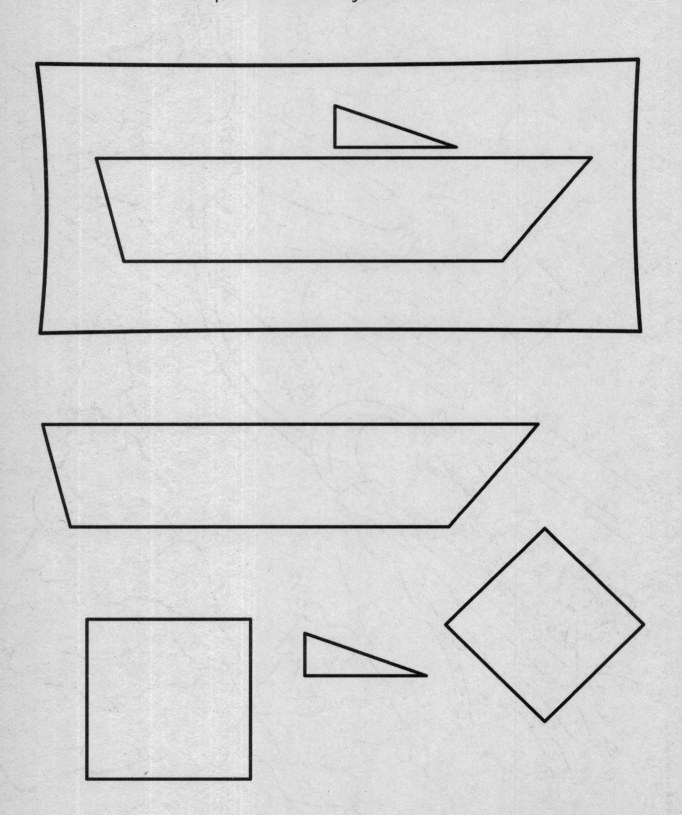

You found the triangle and the trapezoid! Now let's turn this into a super speedboat! *Super Shapes!*

We made it to Iceberg Bay! And there's UmiCar!

The iceberg is melting! Can you help us make UmiCar into a helicopter so he can fly? We need to build a propeller. How many trapezoids do we need?

We rescued UmiCar! I feel a celebration coming on!

2, 4, 6, 8! Everybody Crazy Shake!

Hi, I'm Bot!

This is Milli and her brother, Geo!

We're Team Umizoomi! And we've got
Mighty Math Powers!

Geo and Milli are having so much fun roller-skating.
I would love to go with them!

Can you help me find a pair of roller skates?

Whoa! I'm going so fast, I can't stop! These are crazy skates! I need your help!

UmiFriend, will you help us rescue Bot?
Team Umizoomi, it's time for action!

Uh-oh! Bot is heading for the street fair! Something fell on Bot's head! Connect the dots to find out what is on his head.

Now Bot is heading for the pet store.

Some of the animals are out of their cages and blocking our path. We'll have to use our Pattern Power to put the animals back in their cages.

Can you complete the pattern? Draw the missing animals.

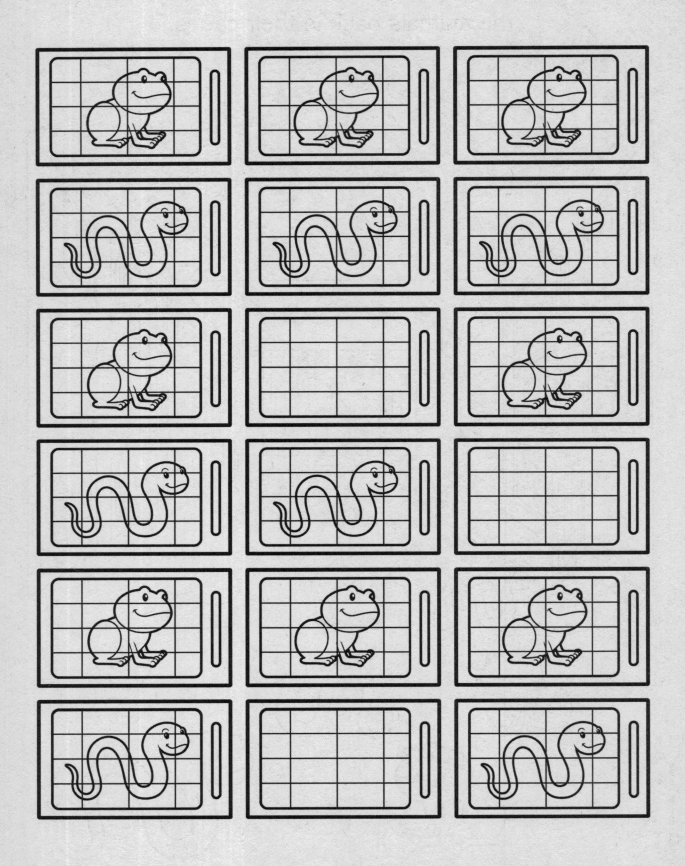

The animals are back in their cages! Now we can get across. Great job, UmiFriend!

Come on, UmiFriend! We've got a robot to rescue!

Oh, no! Something fell on my head and I can't see!

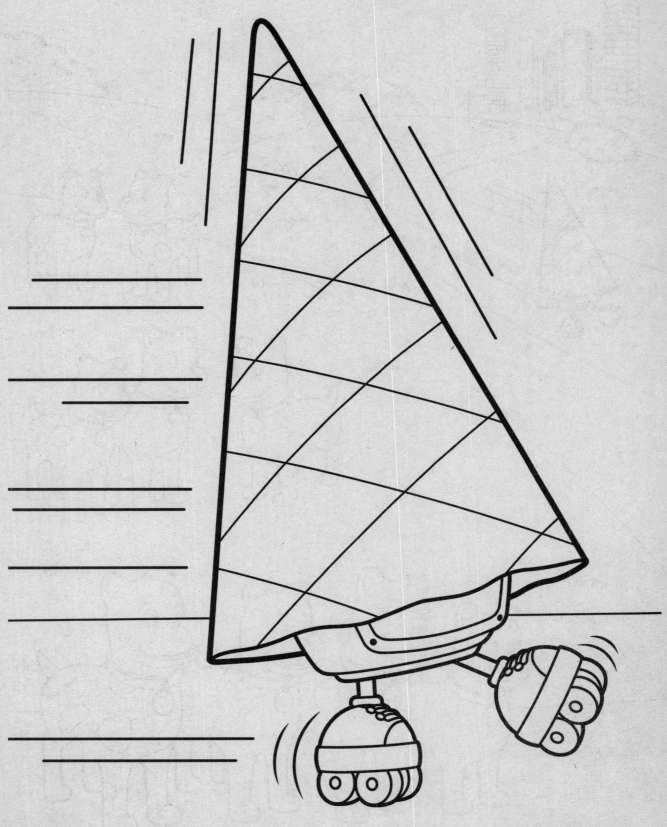

Woof! Woof! Woof! Woof! I hear some dogs.
How many dogs are there?

Great job, UmiFriend!

Ring! Ring! It's the UmiPhone!

It's Bot. He says he's heading to a store that has tents, flashlights, and sleeping bags. Which store would sell those things?

You found the camping store! And there goes Bot on his crazy skates!

Now Bot is in a shop that has dough, cheese, and tomato sauce. Do you know where Bot is?

Hooray! You found the pizza shop. And look—
there goes Bot!

Whoa! I can't stop these crazy skates!

Oh, no! Bot's going to roll right off the roof! I know—
we'll make a big bowl of spaghetti and meatballs for him
to land in. We can make them with my Super Shapes!

We need to make a bowl with a shape that is flat on top and round on the bottom. Color that shape orange!

We need to make spaghetti that is long and wavy.
Color that shape yellow!

Now we need three small circles for meatballs.
Color those shapes brown!

Super Shapes! Our spaghetti and meatballs are ready!
Now let's catch Bot!

Milli and Geo, you saved me! Mmm! Spaghetti!

It's so good to have you back, Bot! Now let's get these skates off once and for all!

Thanks for all your help, UmiFriend!
I feel a celebration coming on!
2, 4, 6, 8! Everybody Crazy Shake!

Mighty! Mighty!
Mighty Math Powers!

We're Team Umizoomi!
And we've got Mighty Math Powers!

Hi, I'm Milli! I can make any pattern with my dress!
Draw lines to connect the dresses that match.

Hi, I'm Bot! You can draw anything on my Belly, Belly, Bellyscreen. What do you want to draw?

Hi, I'm Geo! Check out this cool kite! I made it with shapes! There's a rectangle, an octagon, and three triangles.

Oh, no! The wind blew our kite apart! We need to fix it so we can fly it at the Kite Festival today.

UmiFriend, we're really going to need your help to find the pieces and fix the kite. Team Umizoomi, it's time for action!

UmiCar can help, too. To make UmiCar go really fast,
say "Umi . . . zoomi!"

To find the first piece of the kite, we need to follow the path that shows the numbers in the correct order.

The first piece we need to find is shaped like a rectangle.

Mr. Hummingbird says he saw a rectangle fly into those trees. We need to get up there!

I can build a helicopter with shapes from my ShapeBelt!

Will you draw a circle to finish our blueprint?

Super Shapes! UmiFriend, we made a super helicopter!
I really like building with you.

Now let's fly up, up, up and find that rectangle!

When you see the rectangle, color it green.
You found the rectangle! You're a great shape finder!

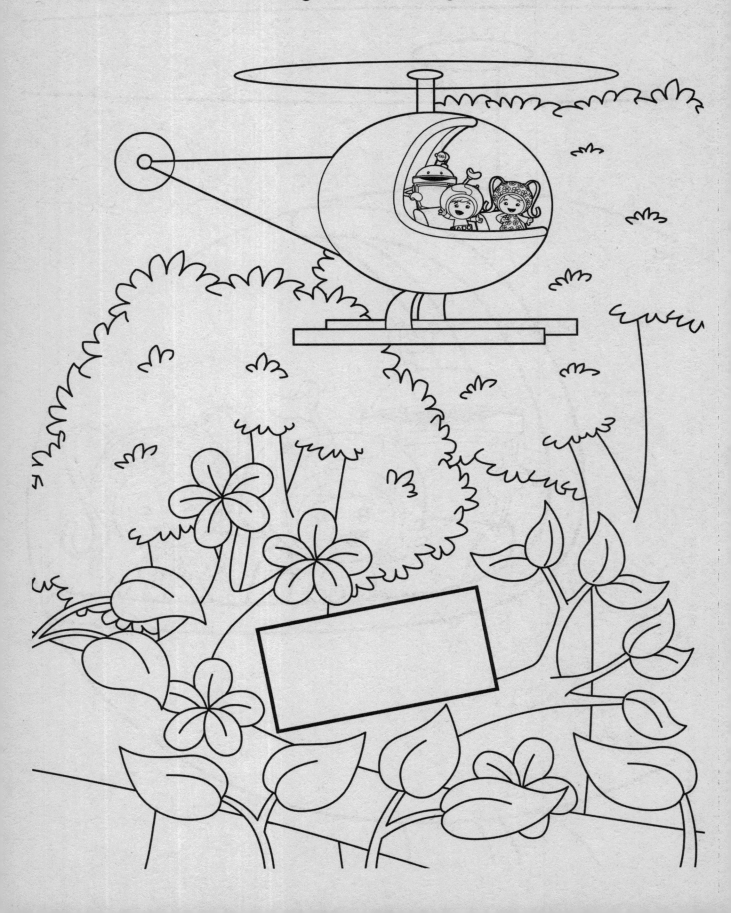

The next piece we have to find is the octagon.

Webster the Spider knows all about octagons. An octagon has 8 sides, and Webster has 8 legs. Webster saw an octagon fly toward those buildings!

Webster said the octagon flew to the top of the tallest building. Which building is the tallest? Color it green.

We made it to the top of the tallest building. Now let's find the octagon. Color the octagon orange. You found the octagon! You're great at spotting shapes!

We still need to find the last 3 pieces of the kite—
the triangles! Look, there go the 3 triangles!
We have to catch them!

The triangles landed on a big billboard. Help us figure out which path will get us to the billboard!

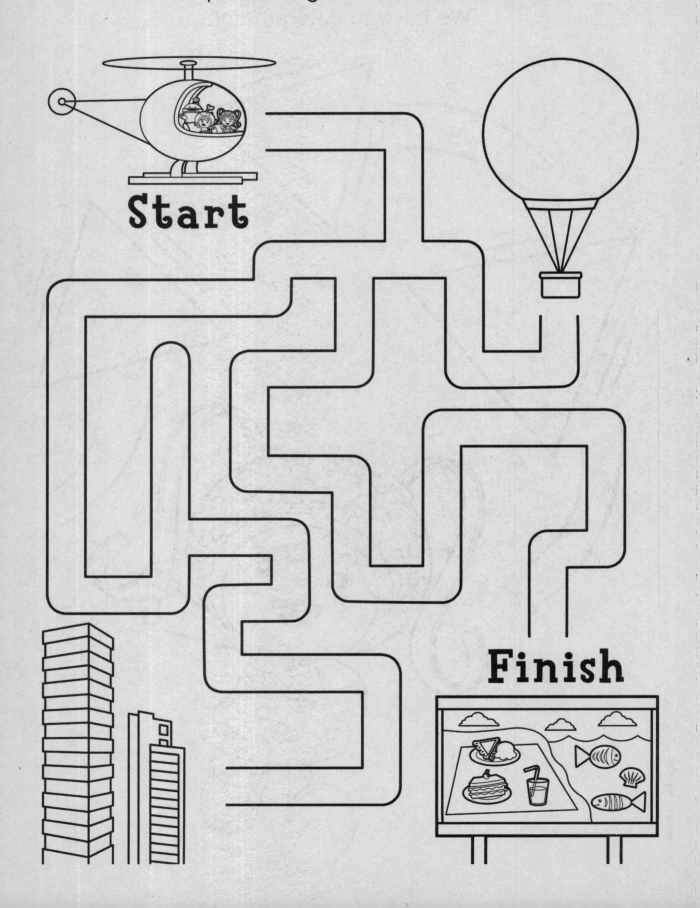

I can climb the billboard with my gear.
Will you connect the dots to make my rope?

● 1

● 2

● 3

4

Do you see a triangle hidden in this picture?
Color it yellow. Great job! We found the first triangle.

Can you find the last 2 triangles hidden in this picture?
Color them yellow.
Thanks, UmiFriend! You found the last 2 triangles!

UmiFriend, we need you to make the kite string!
Draw a line to connect all the pieces and finish the kite.

We made it to the Kite Festival! Look at the great kites!
Color all the shapes you can find.

Let's make more kites. Will you decorate a kite for Bot?

UmiFriend, you're mighty good at math.
We're so glad you're on our team!

Let's go for a kite ride!

UmiFriend, thanks for helping us find all the pieces of the kite. We couldn't have done it without you!

I feel a celebration coming on! Mighty! Mighty! Mighty Math Powers!